THE CHILDREN'S CLASSICS Collection

Dados Internacionais de Catalogação na Publicação (CIP) de acordo com ISBD

L847t London, Jack.
The Call of the Wild / Jack London. - Jandira, SP : W. Books, 2025.
120 p. : 12,80cm x 19,80cm. - (Classics).

ISBN: 978-65-5294-118-3

1. Literatura americana. 2. Aventura. 3. História. 4. Clássicos. I. Título. II. Série.

2025-2482 CDD 810
CDU 821.111-3

Elaborada por Lucio Feitosa - CRB-8/8803
Índice para catálogo sistemático:
1. Literatura americana 810
2. Literatura americana 821.111-3

Text based on the original story by Jack London,
adapted by Gemma Barder
Illustrations by Arianna Bellucci

1st edition in 2025
www.cirandacultural.com.br

The Call of the Wild

Jack London

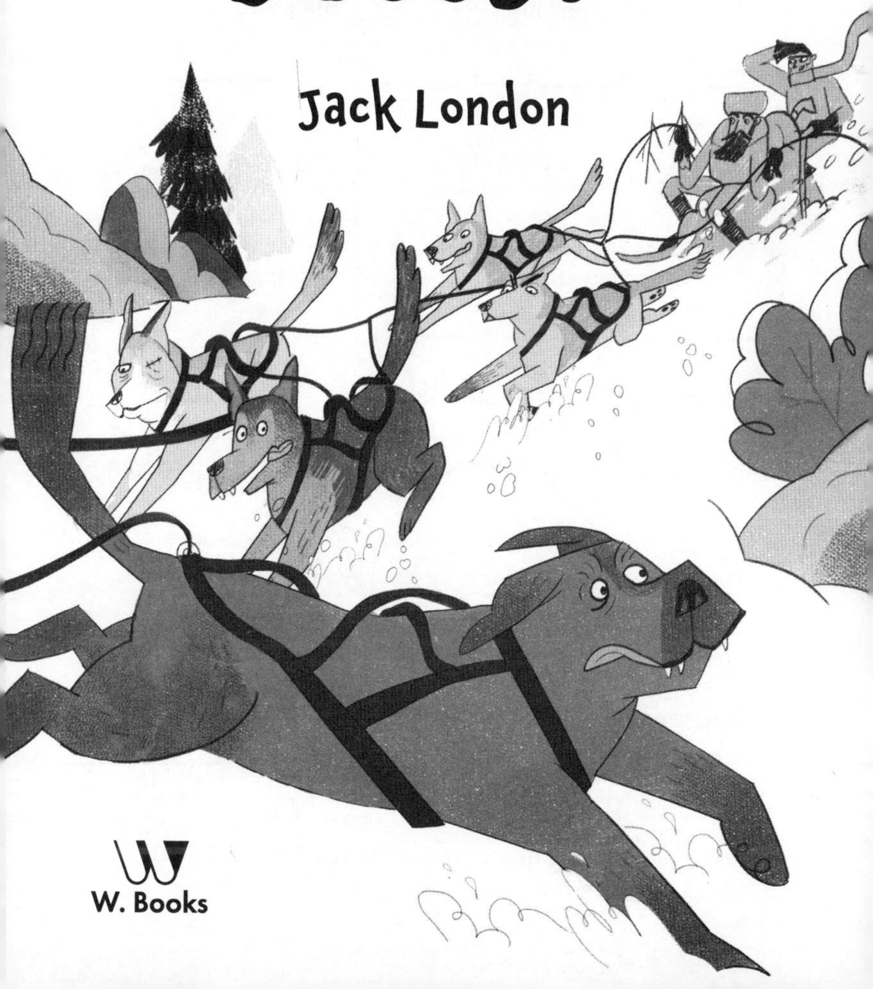

W. Books

The dogs

Buck
Dog taken from home to start a new life

Spitz
Lead sled dog in Buck's team

Dave
Older sled dog in Buck's team

Sol-lek
Older sled dog in Buck's team

Joe
Sled dog in Buck's team

Billee
Sled dog in Buck's team

Curly
Dog who was taken, like Buck

The humans

Judge Miller
Buck's first owner

Manuel
Gardener at Judge Miller's house

The man in the red jumper
Cruel man selling stolen dogs

Perrault and Francois
Postal sled drivers

The Driver
Buys the sled dogs from Perrault and Francois

Hal, Charles and Mercedes
Inexperienced sled drivers who want to find gold

John Thornton
Man who rescues Buck from Hal, Charles and Mercedes

Chapter One

Buck lay on his side and stretched his legs on the warm, soft grass. His shiny fur glistened in the afternoon sun. He was perfectly content.

Buck lived in a large house in San Diego, California. His owner, Judge Miller, was a wealthy and well-respected man. Buck had lived with the judge all his life. His father had been the Judge's dog too. He could

San Diego

A city in the US state of California.

not think of anywhere he would rather be, or anywhere else he could belong.

Buck spent his life happily padding about Judge Miller's large home and estate. Some days he would go hunting or fishing with one of the Judge's sons. Other times he would lie at the feet of the Judge's daughters as they entertained guests for afternoon tea on the lawn, waiting for a crust or

cream cake to fall off the table.

On this particular afternoon, he had been treating the Judge's grandchildren to rides on his back.

Buck was a large, long-haired dog. He was a cross between a St Bernard and a Scotch Collie. The St Bernard part of Buck gave him his size and strength. The Scotch Collie in him made him smart and thoughtful.

Although more than one dog lived at Judge Miller's estate, Buck was the king. It was Buck who

Scotch Collie
A long-haired dog that was used for herding and hunting.

St Bernard
A breed of a very large working dog.

accompanied the Judge on walks into town. It was Buck who had pride of place on the rug in front of the fire each night. It was Buck who the grandchildren fought over to play with.

He was a good-natured, clever dog. However, Buck knew only of his life in San Diego, and the peaceful calm of his home. He did not know that hundreds of miles away, gold had been found in Canada.

The discovery of gold created a gold rush. Hundreds of people

gold rush

The discovery of gold in a certain location that brings a flood of miners to the area, trying to find their fortune.

flocked to Canada in search of their fortune. It was this rush that made dogs like Buck very valuable, as they were built to survive harsh, cold conditions.

Buck lifted his head off the grass and lazily watched the grandchildren as they were scooped up and ordered inside for dinner. The sun was beginning to set and Buck thought about going inside to see what the cook had made for dinner. There were sure to be delicious scraps set aside for him.

As he got to his feet and stretched his legs once more, he noticed Manuel, one of the gardeners, was coming towards him.

Chapter Two

The gardeners liked Buck and often stopped to scratch his ears or give him a pat. Buck was not in the least bit worried when Manuel slipped a rope around his neck and led him towards the woodland. Buck knew the Judge was going out that evening to a meeting. Perhaps the Judge had asked Manuel to take him for a stroll?

Manuel led Buck further and further away from Judge Miller's estate. The sun had set and the evening grew colder. Soon, they came to a small station for freight trains. Manuel glanced down at Buck. 'I'm sorry, fella,' he said. 'But I have debts to pay and a family to feed. I need the money you're going to make me.'

Suddenly, Buck was struck with an unfamiliar feeling. He was unsure and unsafe. A man he had never seen before jumped down from one of the freight train's wooden carriages.

freight train

Trains used to transport cargo rather than passengers.

‘Is this the one?’ said the man. Manuel nodded. The man was tall and wore a dirty, red jumper. He crouched down and looked Buck in the eye. Buck felt his fur bristle. He did not like this man. His instincts

told him that this man wasn't to be trusted. 'You weren't wrong, he's a fine beast,' said the man in the red jumper. 'Here you go. A deal is a deal.' Manuel took a pouch of coins from the man and handed over the rope.

Buck pulled on the rope, trying to follow Manuel. But the man in the red jumper pulled harder, dragging Buck towards the train.

The harder he pulled, the tighter the rope became around Buck's neck. Although he didn't want to, Buck followed the man to avoid the pain of the rope. He jumped onto the train when the man started to drag him in.

The next morning, Buck woke up and realised he was still on the bare

wooden train carriage. But now, it was moving. He had woken up throughout the night as more dogs were loaded onto the carriage.

Each time the wooden doors opened, his ears pricked in the hope that Judge Miller or one of his sons had come to fetch him. But no one came.

He had not eaten or drank water for many hours and his throat felt dry and sore from the rope. The man in the red jumper did not seem to care about any of the dogs he had bought. Buck wondered why he needed so many.

After what felt like countless hours, the train screeched to a halt. The man in the red jumper opened the carriage. 'Come on now, move it!' he ordered. Some of the dogs jumped obediently down from the train. Others cowered in the corner, trembling. Buck stood for a moment, working out what the best thing to do was. He knew the man in the red jumper could not be trusted, but he was confused. The man held a long, wooden club in his hand. What was it for?

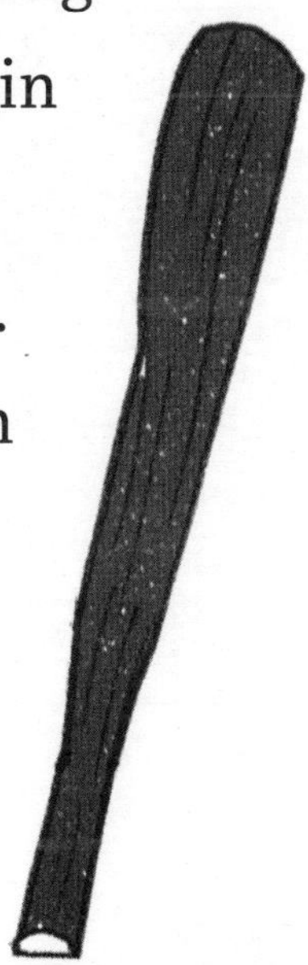

The man took quick steps towards Buck and lunged for the rope around his neck. Instinctively, Buck growled at the man and snapped at him to warn him off. Then, Buck felt something he had rarely experienced in the four years he had been alive. Pain.

The man in the red jumper had hit him with the club. Buck was shocked and dazed. No one had ever treated him this way. All he knew was that he did not want to feel that pain again. When the man in the red jumper raised the club once more, Buck shot out of the train carriage and obediently joined the group of dogs outside.

Chapter Three

It was cold and raining. The air smelt of nothing Buck recognised. It was salty. Even the sky looked different. He knew that he was far away from home. As his long fur slowly became heavy with rain, he watched as all kinds of men came to inspect the dogs. A few times, men came over and whistled an impressed sound when they saw Buck. The man in the red jumper would tell them a price, then they would shake their heads and back away. Buck understood that he was being sold again. The man in the red jumper wanted a high price for him.

Soon, two men came over to Buck and looked him over. One man was short and stocky with a lined, weather-beaten face. His name was Perrault. The other was tall and strong and spoke with a thick, French accent. His name was Francois.

'He's one in a hundred, this one,' said Perrault to the man in the red jumper, unsmiling. 'I've never seen a dog in such good shape. Strong, too.'

The man in the red jumper did not have time to chat. He told Perrault the price. 'That's a mighty high price tag,' said Perrault. 'Luckily we're paying with the government's money, not our own.' Perrault dug deep into his satchel and

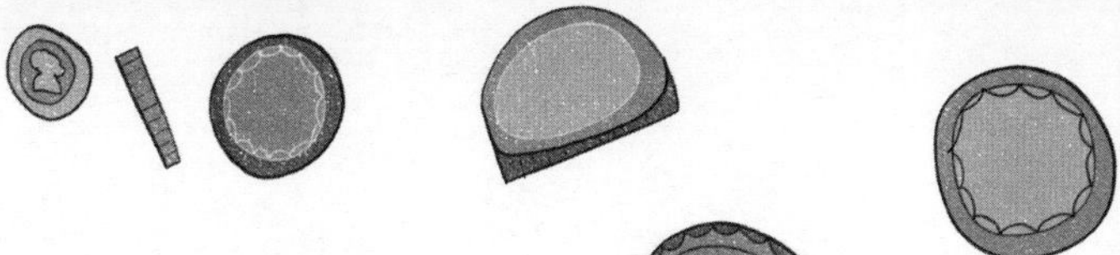
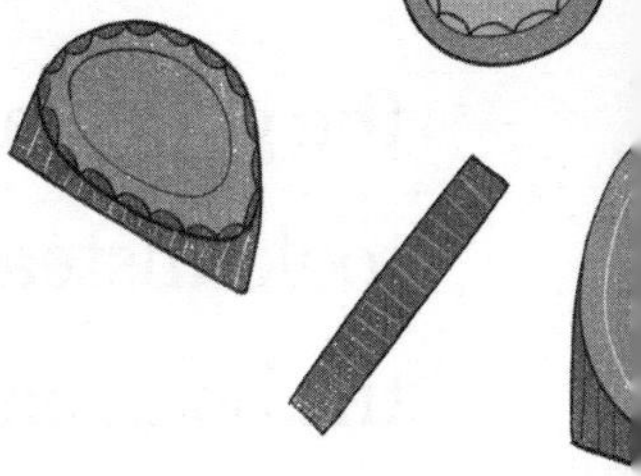
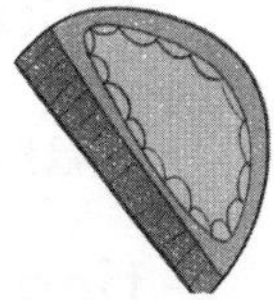

counted the coins into the man in the red jumper's hand.

The man tossed the rope into Perrault's hand. 'His name's Buck, apparently,' he said. And with that, he walked away. Buck was not sad to see the back of him.

Perrault handed the rope to Francois who was already holding the lead of another dog. It was a large Newfoundland called Curly. Together, they walked to

Newfoundland

A large working dog originally from North America.

the gangplank of a boat. Buck took unsteady steps as he boarded the boat, encouraged by the firm guidance of Francois. Buck and Curly were taken below deck and tied up next to two more dogs.

Spitz was a large, snow-white dog. At first, he seemed friendly. But when Francois appeared with bowls of food for each dog, Spitz greedily stole from Buck.

The other dog was called Dave. He acted as though the other dogs did not exist. When they set sail, Buck

gangplank

A moveable plank of wood used to board or leave a ship.

and Curly struggled to keep their balance as the boat rocked against the waves. Buck felt as though the ground was turning to liquid under his paws. Dave, however, simply yawned and took a nap.

After Buck had eaten the food Spitz had not managed to steal from him, and lapped up a bowl full of water, he started to feel stronger. He rested next to Curly, who he suspected would need protection from Spitz. She was too friendly for this strange new world they had found themselves in.

Chapter Four

When the boat finally stopped moving, Perrault and Francois took the dogs up on deck. The first thing that hit Buck was the biting cold. San Diego was never cold, not even in the winter. A strange, soft rain fell from the sky and stuck to Buck's fur in white clumps. When he stepped off the gangplank, his feet sank into a wet, white mush. This was Buck's first experience of snow, but he was soon to know it very well.

They had arrived at a place called Dyea Beach. It was as unlike Judge Miller's home as any place on earth. There were packs of dogs everywhere, sleds filled with cargo and men selling and exchanging tools. And everywhere was white with thick snow and ice. Buck was so hypnotised by the scene that he did not notice Curly wandering over to a group of huskies. As he turned his head, he saw as she tried to nudge them and say hello in her friendly manner. Buck could see their fur

cargo

Goods being transported a great distance.

was bristling. They snapped at her and started to fight. Buck tried to help, but Francois held him back as Perrault stepped in to help Curly.

The dogs had been too strong for Curly. She was too badly hurt to go on. Buck was shocked. He had never seen a pack of dogs behave that way before. He looked at Spitz and Dave. Dave's face was expressionless, but Spitz had laughter in his eyes. From that moment on, Buck decided that Spitz was a cruel dog.

Later, Francois and Perrault brought more dogs to join Buck, Spitz and Dave. Among them were two husky brothers called Joe and Billee. Although they were brothers, they could not have been more different. Joe was grumpy and liked to snarl at anyone who came too close, while Billee was good natured. Finally, there was a husky called Sol-lek. Sol-lek looked older than the rest of the dogs, but just as strong. He was missing one eye and would lash out at anyone who stood on his blind side.

That night, Francois and Perrault set up camp on the beach. They gave the dogs some food, but it was less than half of what Buck was used to. His stomach growled. He could smell food inside Perrault and Francois's tent. But when he tried to go in, he was shooed out into the cold. Where was he to sleep, if not in the tent? He longed for Judge

Miller's warm fire. The thought of it made him even colder.

Then, he noticed Billee digging in the snow. He saw that the rest of the dogs had each dug themselves a little nest of snow to sleep in. Billee showed Buck what to do and, to his surprise, he found the snow hole to be quite cosy. Exhausted from a day of new and strange experiences, Buck fell into a deep sleep.

Chapter Five

The following morning, Buck shook the snow that had fallen overnight from his back and stretched. The sun had come up, but it was still bitterly cold. He was grateful for his long, thick fur. Francois was unloading large, brown sacks from the boat onto a wooden sled. Perrault fiddled with an item made of chains and leather.

'Let's get going!' Perrault called to Francois. 'The mail won't deliver itself!' Francois and Perrault had been employed by the Canadian government to deliver letters and parcels. Thanks to the gold rush, there were hundreds more people making camps along the ice path. It stretched from Salt Water, where they were to begin their journey, to a place called Dawson.

Buck was shocked when Perrault attached him to a harness, just like the ones they put around the horses that pulled Judge Miller's carriage.

The harness was attached to the sled. Buck could see that Spitz was standing proudly at the front of the team of dogs, with Dave, Buck and Sol-lek behind. Billee and Joe were at the back.

Buck knew that he had to run when Francois shouted: 'Mush!' But that was all. He was not used to being in a harness. He was not used to pulling a sled. He stumbled and got tangled in the straps. He often tried to go in a different direction to the other dogs.

mush

An instruction for sled dogs to move. Adopted from the French 'marche', meaning 'go', by English-speaking sled drivers.

Soon, Buck realised why he had been placed between Dave and Sol-lek. The two older dogs, who had been quiet and reserved, came alive when the harness was placed on them. They knew exactly what they were doing. While Spitz was fast and powerful at the lead, the older dogs were experienced. They knew when to lean left and when to lean right. Their legs worked in time like the wheels of a train. When Buck went wrong, they nipped at his heels to correct him. By the end of that first, exhausting day, Buck had learnt so much.

'You've worked well, my boy,' Francois said, patting Buck on the head. He then inspected the pads on each of Buck's paws. They were sore from the cold. Buck's paws were used to soft grass, expensive carpets and polished wooden floors. It would take a while for them to become tough like Dave's and Sol-lek's.

Day after day, the sled powered on through snowdrifts and over frozen rivers. Once or twice, the ice would crack and the dogs had to scramble backwards from the freezing water.

The dogs began to work together like a machine, and soon Buck started to feel his muscles grow stronger. His body learnt to live off the food he was given and, although it surprised him, he started to enjoy running alongside the other dogs.

Somehow, he knew that this was what his body was built for. Perhaps not to pull a sled, but to survive in the cold, to run and feel powerful.

Chapter Six

One night, when Perrault and Francois were cooking their dinner over a campfire, Buck heard a noise. It felt familiar, yet he had never heard it before. A low, threatening howl, too far away for his human masters to hear.

He glanced around and saw that Dave, Spitz, Joe and Sol-lek had heard it too. Billee was dozing, but soon he raised his head as well. Buck growled as his eyes scanned the dark horizon. Something was coming closer.

The camp had been surrounded by wild huskies. They were thin, and obviously hungry. Their noses had caught the scent of Perrault and Francois's supper cooking on the fire. Each sled dog snarled at the intruders. There was a moment of tense stillness. Then all around was chaos.

Some of the huskies went for the food. Others began to fight with the sled dogs. Perrault and Francois used their clubs to warn off the huskies in the camp.

Then they ran over to help their own dogs. As Buck fought alongside the rest of his team, he felt a pair of jaws clamp around his leg. He was shocked to see that it was not a wild husky, but Spitz.

Spitz's eyes gleamed up at Buck. He knew that this was his chance to show Buck who was in charge. With the fight whirling all around them, Spitz wanted to hurt Buck and frighten him into submission.

But Buck was strong, and he was not about to let Spitz get the better of him. He managed to kick his legs free of Spitz's jaws. Before Buck could strike back, Perrault and Francois had frightened the wild huskies away. The dogs and their masters stood and panted in the snow. Their camp was a mess, and all of the dogs were injured.

Francois inspected each dog and tried to patch up their wounds, while Perrault checked the sled.

The team still had miles to go before they reached Dawson and they could not waste time resting. The following morning, they carried on their journey. Buck locked eyes with Spitz whenever he could. He needed to show Spitz that he was not scared by his attack.

Soon, Buck's paws became so sore that Francois cut the leather from the top of his own boots to make little shoes for him. Even Perrault could not help but smile as Francois popped the shoes on Buck each morning like a devoted father. However, over time, Buck's feet grew as hard as the rest of the team's and he no longer needed them.

Spitz carried on threatening Buck. When Perrault and Francois weren't looking, he would take a bite at Buck, or shoulder-shove him so that he lost his balance. No matter how big and strong Buck was, and no matter how well he pulled the sled, Spitz was determined to show that he was still the leader.

Chapter Seven

After hundreds of miles, working together in the ice and snow, the sled finally made it to Dawson. There were hundreds of dogs in the town. They pulled machinery and two-man sleds, as well as sleds heavy with cargo like their own.

It was here that the dogs were finally allowed to rest. But Spitz would not stop tormenting Buck. When Perrault and Francois had found a place to camp, the dogs dug their little nests, intending to sleep for the night.

Spitz wanted to show the rest of the group that he was in charge, whether they were pulling the sled or at rest. He picked the weakest member of the group, Billee, and got ready to pounce on him to show them all who was boss.

Buck could see what was happening. He had been thinking for some time that Spitz should not be a leader of any group. Spitz did not care about the team; he only cared about himself. In fact,

Buck believed that it was his own destiny to take charge. He could feel it inside him. He cared about the pack, where Spitz only cared about keeping control. Buck knew he could use his strength to motivate all of the sled dogs to do their best. But Spitz only used his strength to scare and intimidate.

Billee whimpered at the sight of Spitz coming towards him with his teeth bared, and Buck sprang to his feet and blocked Spitz's path. With this act, Buck had announced to Spitz, and the rest of the dogs, that he was challenging

him for the leader's spot. He wanted to take control from Spitz.

As Spitz stalked away from the group, snarling with frustration, Buck noticed that Francois had been watching them. The driver shook his head slightly as he looked from Spitz to Buck.

After seven days of rest, Perrault and Francois started to load up the sled once more. Perrault had a spring in his step. 'I reckon we can get this load back to Salt Water in record time,' he said. 'If we beat the record, we'll be given a hero's welcome and a bonus from the post office, too.'

Francois laughed at his friend and shook his head. 'These dogs have worked hard already,' he said. 'Their pace might be slower on the way back.'

'These are some of the best sled dogs I've known!' Perrault said.

'That Buck can really pull.'

While Perrault was in good spirits, there was still one concern on Francois's mind. Francois crouched next to Buck and spoke softly. 'You and Spitz are heading for a fight,' he sighed. 'I can feel it.'

Chapter Eight

As the sled began its journey back to Salt Water, Buck began his campaign against Spitz. Each time Spitz went to bite another member of the team, Buck was there to stop him. If Spitz tried to steal food from another dog's bowl, Buck would growl and bare his teeth at him.

Slowly, Buck got bolder. He would steal food from Spitz. He pulled the sled harder than he ever had. He would show the team, and

Francois and Perrault, who the real leader should be.

One night, as they camped near a forest, a rabbit shot across the path of the sled team. Their natural instincts were too strong to deny and all the dogs ran into the forest after it. Buck was thrilled as he led his pack on the chase, even more than pulling the sled. Buck felt as though this is what he was meant to do.

From the power in his legs, right through to the scent he picked up with his nose – he was alive!

Buck noticed that Spitz had broken away from the group. Spitz had taken a shortcut and got there first, just as the group were about to pounce on the rabbit. The team were disappointed, but Buck was furious. He snorted and his fur bristled. Dave, Sol-lek, Billee and Joe paced backwards. It was time for Buck and Spitz to have the fight they all knew was coming.

A whirl of teeth and fur followed. At first, Buck looked as though he

was beaten. Spitz was strong and used to fighting for his position. But Buck glanced at the faces of the team that were watching him. They'd had enough of Spitz's leadership. They wanted Buck to win. Buck mustered all the strength he could and soon he was fighting back.

'What are y'all doing!' Perrault cried, approaching the dogs. Together with Francois he pulled the dogs apart. Spitz's leg was badly damaged.

'I knew it,' Francois said. 'I just knew these two would have it out one day.'

Back at camp, Francois tended to both dogs' wounds. Buck was scratched, but still strong. Spitz's leg needed to be bandaged.

'Spitz can't lead anymore,' Francois said the following morning, as Perrault prepared the harness. He was annoyed. He wanted to break the record for the fastest journey along the ice path, but without his strongest dog at the lead, it would be impossible. 'We'll just have to leave him behind.'

Buck padded to the front of the harness, ready to take his rightful place as leader. But Francois pulled Sol-lek up front instead. He needed a dog with experience to lead the pack, now that Spitz could not. Buck was strong, but he had only been a sled dog for a few months.

Buck was shaken. He should have been the leader. He wanted it, and he had earned it. Sol-lek backed away from Francois and went back to his position next to Dave. That was his spot and where he knew he belonged. Buck stood firm, refusing to go back to his old position. Francois scratched his head and looked between the two dogs.

'What's the hold up?' Perrault said, marching up from the back of the sled. 'Get these dogs harnessed and let's go!'

'It's ol' Sol-lek,' Francois said. 'He won't lead.'

Perrault shook his head with frustration and went to fetch

something from the sled. Immediately Buck knew what it was. He had seen Perrault use it when the wild huskies had attacked. He had seen it in the hands of the man in the red jumper. It was a club. Buck let out a low growl. He backed away, but still did not take up his old place.

Perrault's eyes met Buck's glare. Eventually he lowered the club and nodded. 'You want to lead, hey? All right then,' Perrault said. He turned to Francois. 'Put Buck in the lead and we'll see what happens.'

But Buck was rooted to the spot, his eyes firmly on the club in Perrault's hand. He remembered the pain of the blow the man in the red jumper had given him. 'Drop the club,' Francois said, looking from Buck to Perrault. 'This one is clever. He knows.'

As Perrault dropped the club with a thump in the snow, Buck stepped forward again. He did not flinch as the harness was put on him. When Francois cried: ‘Mush!’ he pulled stronger and faster than ever before.

Chapter Nine

Perrault and Francois reached Salt Water in a record-breaking time. They were greeted by the other mail teams as heroes. No one had ever seen a run like it. Buck and his team were exhausted, but they knew they were due for a long rest, now that another run was complete.

The morning after they arrived in Salt Water, Buck spotted Francois and Perrault talking to a man in an official-looking uniform. They looked happy and shook hands with the man. Buck was proud that his masters were getting so much praise and attention because of the team he had led. But when Francois came over to Buck, he had tears in his eyes.

Francois put his arms around Buck. 'You've done well, boy,' he said, sniffing. 'I'm going to miss you.'

Perrault helped Francois to his feet and patted his shoulder. 'They'll be fine,' he said, kindly.

'They've done us proud. Now it's time for us to enjoy our time off. They've already got a new team to look after them.'

Francois sniffed, rubbed Buck's ears and patted each dog in turn. Buck noticed that even Joe and Sol-lek leant into Francois's hand fondly. Then, the two men were gone.

Buck, Dave, Sol-lek, Billee and Joe should have been enjoying a well-earned rest. But the man in the uniform had a different plan for them. He had been so impressed with their record-breaking journey from Dawson that he wanted to get them back

out on the snow and ice as soon as possible. He was in charge of getting mail delivered and he decided to give this top team of dogs an even bigger cargo load.

The team was hitched to another sled, with Buck at the lead. The sled was bigger and carried more sacks of mail, so they added more dogs to the team. Although he was tired, Buck soon managed to get the new dogs to follow him as their leader.

They set off once again for Dawson. Although the weather was getting warmer, the ice and snow was still hard on their legs and paws. They tired sooner than they would have if they'd had a proper rest at Salt Water. A few days into their journey, Buck noticed that Dave was acting strangely.

Chapter Ten

The driver of Buck's new team was not an unkind man. He had a job to do, and that job came above anything else. But he treated the dogs well. Because they were on a more important mission, the dogs were fed more food than they had received with Perrault and Francois. But even the extra food was not enough to keep them going.

Dave was the oldest dog on

the team. Buck knew that he had not been the same since the wild husky attack. Though his injuries had healed, he was not as strong as he had once been.

The driver saw this too. One night, he brought Dave to lie by the fire with him, and Buck watched as he checked him over. Dave obediently let the driver inspect his paws and his teeth. The driver sighed. Buck could read the expression on the driver's face and it made his heart sink.

The following morning, the driver fixed all the dogs into the harness apart from Dave. The driver lifted Dave into the sled to sit by him, but Dave was not happy.

Dave had been a sled dog all his life. He came alive in the harness and it made him happy to run with his team. He did not understand what the driver wanted him to do, but he did not like it.

Each time he was lifted onto the sled, he jumped down and padded over to his spot next to Sol-lek. Buck wished the driver could understand. No matter how tired he was, Dave wanted to do his job. Finally, the driver put Dave into his harness and they set back off onto the trail to Dawson. Although he tripped and fell, Dave refused to give up.

When they arrived in Dawson, the team were exhausted. Buck went from dog to dog, padding round them. He gave Billee a playful nudge. When he came to Dave, he saw that he was lying on the ground. All his energy had gone.

He had done what he had wanted to do, right until the end.

Buck remembered the last time his team had been in Dawson. They'd had seven days of blissful rest, with nothing to do but lay about, eat and drink water. With Dave gone, they were all feeling low and looked forward to gaining back their strength.

Two days later, they were being strapped back into their harness. Buck was confused. This wasn't how they worked with Francois and Perrault. His team needed more rest.

Buck took two steps back as the driver came to harness him.

'I know, boy,' the driver sighed, and Buck noticed how tired the driver looked. 'But we gotta get going. If we leave it any later, the weather will only get warmer and some of that ice will start melting. It will be impossible to pass.'

Buck understood. He had seen that parts of the frozen rivers they travelled across had started

to crack. He saw the remains of sleds that had fallen through the ice and he didn't want that to happen to his team. He let the driver place the harness on him, and once again set off on the ice path.

Chapter Eleven

Somehow, Buck and his team of sled dogs found the strength to make it to Salt Water. They had made all their deliveries, but it had come at a cost. Each dog had given their best, and they were now broken and tired. The driver was grateful to the dogs. He knew they could not travel the ice path again – not at the speed the Canadian government needed them to.

The team were sold, once again. This time, they were bought by two people who had come from America to find gold and get rich. Their names were Charles and Hal, and Buck knew straight away that they did not have much experience with sleds or dogs.

Their clothes were more suited to a walk in the park than a hard trek across the Canadian wilds. They argued among themselves, which gave Buck a feeling of dread.

Buck, Sol-lek, Billee and Joe were led to Charles and Hal's camp. Charles was about the same age as Perrault, Buck reckoned. But he looked like he had lived a better life. His face was not as lined, and he looked like he spent most of his time indoors. Hal was younger, with a determined look on his face as he dragged the dogs to camp.

The camp was unlike anything Buck had seen in all his months as a sled dog. Dirty pots lay here and there. Even the tent was pitched at an odd angle rather than straight.

Their sled was packed with oddly shaped bundles. Chairs stuck out of one end with broom handles poking out of the other.

As they approached, a woman came out of the tent and squealed with delight. 'You got them!' she said, running up to the dogs. 'They are so cute!'

'They aren't pets,' said Hal, gruffly. 'They're our transportation. They're goin' to lead us to the gold up in Dawson.'

Buck's heart sank as he realised that they would be heading back up the ice path once again. He remembered what the driver had told him about the weather getting warmer. If an experienced man like the driver was worried, then Buck felt they would have no hope with their new owners.

Buck listened to as much of his new masters' conversation as he could. He learnt that the woman was called Mercedes, and she was married to Charles. Hal was Mercedes's brother. Together, they had left their old lives in America behind. They had set out to find their fortune in gold – as so many others had tried to do.

‘Hal, I was talking to some men earlier today,’ began Charles, as they cooked sausages over the fire that evening. Buck watched on, his stomach grumbling at the scent of the food. ‘They said the ice path is breaking up. It would be a miracle if we made it to Dawson going that way.’

Mercedes looked at her husband with fear, but Hal shook his head. 'They're saying that because they don't want no one else goin' up there and finding the gold!' he said. 'They want it all to themselves.'

Buck miserably padded back to where his team lay sleeping. It was a good thing they were resting, because tomorrow they would be working once again.

Chapter Twelve

Buck stared up at the sled. Mercedes had piled the sled high with everything you could imagine ever needing on a trip.

Travellers from neighbouring camps tried to offer advice about carrying less, but Hal batted them away. He strapped the dogs in as best he could and ordered them to move. Each dog pulled with all their might, as they had done so many times before. But the sled stayed firm.

'They're just being lazy!' Hal cried angrily. He reached into the sled and brought out a horsewhip. The crack of the whip frightened Buck and the dogs into trying once again, but still the sled did not move.

'It's too heavy. Let's take out the things we don't really need,' said Charles, eyeing the sled up and down. Mercedes was horrified. To her, each item was essential, right down to the little potted plant she brought to make the tents feel

horsewhip

A long whip used to steer and control horses.

more like home. After a bit of gentle persuading, the load was lightened. Hal raised his whip again.

'Must you hit the poor dears?' said Mercedes, who still saw the dogs as pets.

'Yes, or else they'll think I'm not their master!' said Hal, beginning to whip each dog in turn.

Slowly, the sled began to move. Hal smiled triumphantly at his sister and brother-in-law, who walked beside the sled. However, Hal did not stop hitting the dogs. Buck's anger grew with each blow that fell on his back. What gave this man the right to hit him and his team?

Soon the road to town started to slope downwards, and the dogs picked up speed. As they rounded a corner, the sled toppled over,

sending Hal and half of the sled's contents flying across the road.

Angry at the team's bad treatment, Buck did not stop running. Sol-lek, Billee and Joe did not stop either. And they would have carried on running, if a group of kind passersby hadn't stopped to help the trio of gold diggers.

Hal was humiliated. He did not speak as they packed up the sled for the third time. They got rid of more items, much to Mercedes's disappointment, and finally headed out onto the melting ice path.

Chapter Thirteen

Buck did not trust his new masters. Since he had arrived in Canada all those months ago, Buck had become a different dog. He had learnt a new way of life. He knew the twists and turns of the mountain trail. He could smell when bad weather was in the air and his paws could sense if the ice was too thin to walk on.

Charles, Hal and Mercedes did not know the land and often

took wrong turns. They pushed the team too hard and always set up camp too late. They did not feed the dogs enough food and expected too much of them. They argued with each other all day long. Buck wished that he could chew through his harness and set his team loose.

Buck could feel his strong muscles withering from lack of food and rest. Sol-lek and Joe were so tired that they forgot about being grumpy and huddled up with the rest of the team at night. Billee whimpered with pain in his sleep.

It was a relief when they spotted a camp ahead of them, where fires burnt and the tents were pitched in the proper way. When the sled stopped, the dogs fell down on the spot, desperate to rest.

A man with a grey beard and woollen hat approached them. 'My name's John Thornton. How can I help you folks?'

'We're headed up the ice path to Dawson,' replied Charles, politely. 'I wonder, do you have any food we could buy from you?'

John Thornton looked over the sled and the dogs. His eyes rested on Buck. 'The ice path is melting. You'll have to find another way if you want to survive the journey,' he said.

Hal scoffed. 'Ha! You're another one who wants to keep the gold for yourself!' he said. 'Come on, let's keep moving.' Charles and Mercedes looked at Hal in disbelief.

'The dogs need to rest, Hal,' Mercedes pleaded.

'They're fine, they just need encouraging,' said Hal, raising his whip.

Buck stood up first and was hit by the whip. His legs buckled and he fell to the ground, exhausted. Hal raised his arm again, but the whip was caught by John Thornton. 'You hit this dog again, and I'll whip you,' he said calmly.

Thornton was taller than Hal, and although he was older, he was far stronger. Hal swallowed nervously. Thornton threw his whip away, but he was too scared to go and get it back.

Thornton undid the harness on Buck and comforted him with his strong arms. 'This one is staying with me. If you know what's good for you, you'll head back along the road. The ice path is no good.'

Hal was angry at this man for taking his dog, but he knew there was nothing he could do. He shouted at the rest of the dogs to get to their feet. Ignoring Thornton's advice, they headed back onto the ice path. Buck had just enough strength to raise his head and watch as the dogs he had been through so much with wearily set off into the distance.

Suddenly, there was a sickeningly loud crack. Buck's ears pricked with fear as he watched the sled slide into the icy water. The ice path had split and the team, with their foolish masters, disappeared underneath. There was nothing Buck or John Thornton could do to help them.

Chapter Fourteen

For the next few weeks, Buck rested. He ate the best food he had tasted since being taken from Judge Miller and he slept each night in the glow of the campfire. Often, he would imagine he was back home, basking in the San Diego sun.

He grew stronger and stronger each day, and each day he grew to love Thornton more and more. He had respected Judge Miller when he had lived with him. But Thornton was a man of the wild. He understood the natural world, too. Buck felt connected to him in a way he had never known he could back in San Diego.

After being left by Perrault, Francois and the driver, Buck wanted to make sure he would not be abandoned again. He followed Thornton faithfully wherever he went.

Thornton had a team of men who efficiently packed up their camp and moved from place to place. They were also on the lookout for gold, but unlike his previous masters, Thornton and his crew were clever and experienced. They sailed along rivers when the ice melted and knew the safest places to camp. For the first time in nearly a year, Buck felt as though he had a home.

Buck was so grateful, that he took every opportunity to watch over his master and keep him safe. When Thornton got into a fight, Buck was there to warn off the attacker. When Thornton fell into the river and almost drowned, it was Buck who swam in to pull him to safety.

One night, Thornton and his crew were eating dinner in a saloon. Buck was nearby, watching on. 'That's one fine dog you have there,' said the saloon keeper. 'Never seen a dog so big and strong.'

Thornton nodded. 'He can pull a sled real good, too. I bet he could pull 1,000 pounds if you tried him.'

The saloon keeper laughed. 'Never!' he said. 'I bet you 1,000 dollars he can't do it.'

saloon
An establishment that serves drinks.

pounds
A weight measurement commonly used in the United States, abbreviated as 'lbs'.

dollars
The currency of the United States of America.

Thornton looked between Buck and the crew. 'You're on,' he said.

Soon, Buck was fastened to a sled that contained 1,000 pounds of flour. Although he had no idea what amount he was about to pull, or the amount of money that was at stake, he knew something important was about to happen. He felt the excitement build up in his muscles.

Thornton crouched down next to Buck and rubbed his ears. He placed his forehead to Buck's and whispered, 'Come on, boy. You can do it.'

Buck could feel the men from the saloon watching him, but he did not look at them. He stared straight ahead and kept his eyes on Thornton. He wanted to show Thornton how grateful he was for rescuing and for taking such good care of him. He dug his paws into the ground and willed all his muscles to work together. Inch-by-inch the sled began to move. Soon it gained momentum. Everyone was whooping and cheering him on. Everyone, apart from the saloon keeper – who had to part with 1,000 dollars.

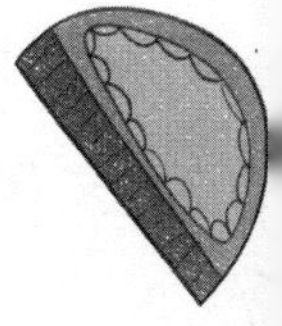

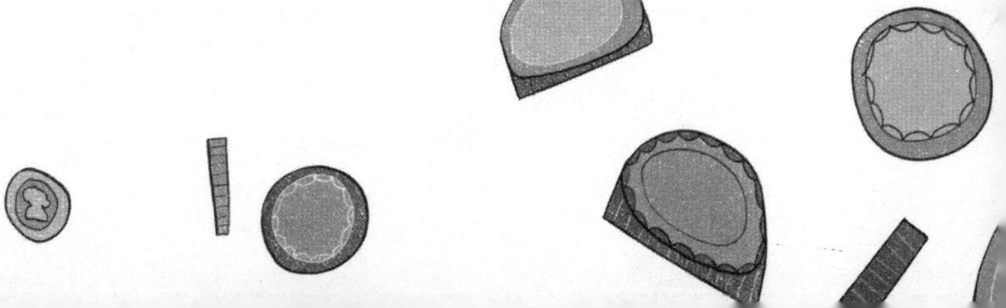

Chapter Fifteen

The money Buck had won for Thornton meant that his crew could head out to the east of Canada. It was rumoured that there was an old gold mine there, yet to be discovered. The crew were cheerful, knowing that they had the money to travel and eat well. Each night, they would camp and Buck would fall asleep in the glow of the campfire.

Now and then, Buck remembered the thrill he felt while chasing the rabbit all that time ago, and he would head out into the forest to hunt. He loved the excitement of spotting a creature and chasing it.

As time went on, Buck found that he was being pulled in two directions. Part of him wanted to stay with Thornton – to be looked after, fed and petted. Another part of him wanted to run wild and free.

One night, when the camp was asleep, Buck heard a familiar sound. It was a howl, like the wild huskies, but lower. He felt like it was calling to him. He scampered into the forest and there, in a clearing, was a wolf. Buck was not afraid. He stared at the silvery wolf and approached it slowly. He wanted the wolf to know that he meant it no harm. Although the wolf was cautious at first, he soon started to play with Buck. They chased each other through the

trees, hunted together and howled at the moon. Buck felt happy and alive.

When Buck heard his name being called, he instinctively darted back towards the camp. 'Where've you been?' Thornton said, rubbing his head. 'I think you must be part wolf, the way you carry on.'

Buck was pleased that they had set up camp by the forest for a while. Thornton and his crew were searching for gold in the river and that would take time. Buck spent his days padding around the camp, keeping Thornton company and being fed. At night, he would go to the forest to find the wolf. The times he spent running wild and free in the forest were his happiest. In those moments, everything was just as it should be.

One night, the wolf took Buck to meet his pack. He was nervous to see so many wolves all in one spot. At first, they circled him and bared their teeth. Buck did not react, and stood firm with his head held high.

He had to show them he was not a threat, but that he was not afraid of them either. The following night, he brought the pack some food he had hunted. He placed it on a rock and stood back for them to take it.

Soon, the pack accepted him. His size, strength and intelligence meant that it would be better to have Buck on their side, as their leader. One night, Buck stayed with the pack far longer than he had ever stayed away from camp before. When morning came, there was no call from Thornton.

Chapter Sixteen

Buck padded through the forest, back to camp. He felt a kind of loss each time he left the wolves. He had started to think of them as family – more so than Dave, Sol-lek, Joe and Billee had ever felt to him.

As he stepped out of the forest, Buck could sense that something had gone wrong. The camp was a mess. The tents had been torn down and there was chaos everywhere. Buck sniffed furiously, looking for Thornton among the debris.

Then, Buck spotted arrows. He had heard Thornton and his men talk of a native tribe who lived in the woods. They did not like people invading their land and taking from it. Whatever

had happened here was not good. Thornton and his crew had disappeared, and Buck could find no trace of his master's scent.

Buck howled mournfully. He had loved Thornton more than he had ever loved any human.

Thornton had rescued him, and Buck had not been around to help him when he needed it.

He nudged the bowls and crates of food and lapped at the water at the river's edge.

He felt completely alone. As he looked up from the river, he spotted his wolf friend poking his long snout out between the trees. Bravely, the wolf approached the camp.

The wolf gently nudged Buck's shoulder and licked his face. Buck knew then that he had found his family. A pack that would be his forever. He would have no master, and no one could sell him whenever it took their fancy.

Soon, more of the pack came to join Buck in the deserted camp. They surrounded him and sat beside him. Some howled, some played in the water. Then, all at once, they began to run. And Buck ran with them.

Epilogue

For years, those who searched for gold in the east of Canada would talk of a 'ghost dog'. He was far bigger than a wolf, but too wild to be a domestic dog. He ran with a pack of wolves and knew where the humans liked to camp. He stole food and ran fast. Everyone who spotted him said the same thing. He looked full of life, and happy.

Jack London

Jack London was born in California in 1876. He quit school at fourteen to travel. London went as far as Japan before returning to the United States. With so much travelling and job-hopping, it led him to struggle to make money. This is when London turned to writing stories. His first book, published in 1900, *The Son of the Wolf: Tales of the Far North* gained a wide audience. This success let to *The Call of the Wild* being published in 1903.